The Race Across Anaconda Swamp

A Challenge Island
STEAM Adventure

By Sharon Duke Estroff and Joel Ross

Illustrated by Mónica de Rivas

WEST
MARGIN
PRESS

Edited by Michelle McCann

Library of Congress Cataloging-in-Publication Data

Names: Estroff, Sharon, author. | Ross, Joel N., 1968- author. |
    Rivas, Monica de, illustrator.
Title: The race across Anaconda Swamp : a Challenge Island STEAM adventure
    / by Sharon Duke Estroff and Joel Ross ; illustrated by Mónica de Rivas.
Description: [Berkeley, CA] : West Margin Press, [2022] | Series: Challenge
    Island ; book 2 | Audience: Ages 7-10 | Audience: Grades 2-3 | Summary:
    After finding themselves mysteriously transported to a magical island,
    this time in a rainforest swamp, Daniel, Joy, and Kimani must figure out
    how to safely traverse across the island with their knowledge of friction
    and pulleys.
Identifiers: LCCN 2021052470 (print) | LCCN 2021052471 (ebook) |
    ISBN 9781513128702 (paperback) | ISBN 9781513128719 (hardback) |
    ISBN 9781513128726 (ebook)
Subjects: LCSH: Rain forests--Fiction. | CYAC: Islands--Fiction. |
    Swamps--Fiction. | Cooperativeness--Fiction. | Resourcefulness--Fiction.
    | Problem solving
Classification: LCC PZ7.1.E854 Rac 2022 (print) | LCC PZ7.1.E854 (ebook) |
    DDC [Fic]--dc23
LC record available at https://lccn.loc.gov/2021052470
LC ebook record available at https://lccn.loc.gov/2021052471

LS2022

Published by West Margin Press®

WEST
MARGIN
PRESS
WestMarginPress.com

Proudly distributed by Ingram Publisher Services

WEST MARGIN PRESS
Publishing Director: Jennifer Newens   Editor: Olivia Ngai
Marketing Manager: Alice Wertheimer   Design & Production:
Project Specialist: Micaela Clark   Rachel Lopez Metzger
                                         Design Intern: Qilu Zhou

Dear Reader,

Welcome to Challenge Island, a magical place where engineering meets imagination! You are about to set sail on an exhilarating voyage to one of the many action-packed Challenge Islands. Each island comes with a unique set of problems that the Challenge Island kids have to solve—together! They have to be creative, using only what's in the treasure chest and their imaginations. After the story, at the back of the book, you will have a chance to try out the challenges with your own team at home!

Boom. Boom. Boom. Did you hear that? It sounds like the Challenge Island drums calling you. That means the adventure is about to begin. *Boom. Bada-boom!* There it is again. Sounds like it's time for us to get going full STEAM ahead!

Happy reading!
Sharon Duke Estroff
Co-Author and Founder/
CEO of the Challenge Island STEAM Program

Chapter 1

"**W**hat are *you* doing here?" Joy's sister asked from the kitchen doorway.

"I live here," Joy said as she tapped a rhythm on the table with a spoon. "Remember?"

"And I'm eating pizza," Daniel said, his mouth full of crust.

"Eating my *birthday* pizza!" Joy's sister narrowed her eyes. "My party's about to start and you two are *not invited*. Go away!"

"Fine." Joy stood. "C'mon, Daniel."

"We're leaving?" Daniel asked, surprised that Joy

was giving in so easily.

"Yeah, that's the birthday gift I'm giving her. Us being gone."

"Oh," he said, and followed Joy across the apartment.

Her ponytail swayed and her chunky blue hair tie bobbed when she walked. As she opened the front door, she explained to Daniel, "This way, I don't have to make her a card."

"You love making cards," he said.

"Not when she's being a jerk," Joy said, stepping into the hallway.

Daniel swallowed the last bite of his fourth slice of pizza. "So, what now?"

Instead of answering, Joy drummed a rhythm on the closed door and sang, "Boom-bada-boom-di-boom."

"That's not going to work," Daniel told her.

"It—boom-da-boom—might!"

Joy had been drumming nonstop for weeks. She thumped everything she saw—including random dogs in the street—because she thought the right rhythm would *whoosh* her and Daniel away to a magical tropical island. Which wasn't as silly as it sounded;

that had actually happened to them last month, and they'd ended up on Sharktooth Island.

Still, Daniel was pretty sure it wouldn't happen again.

"No, it boom-da-boom won't," he told Joy. "Would you give up already?"

"Never!" she cried as she drummed a quick *rat-a-tat*.

Daniel groaned, because it was true: Joy never gave up. Nobody knew that better than he did. He and Joy were cousins, and they'd been best friends since before they could walk. That's why the family called them the twins, even though Daniel was big for his age with dark hair and dark eyes while Joy was a shrimp with reddish hair and blue eyes.

"I'm so close," Joy said, patting the wall as they headed toward the elevator.

"To what? You've been drumming for weeks and we're still here."

"Yeah." Joy fiddled with her beaded necklace, a souvenir from their last adventure. "I wonder what Kimani's doing."

"She's probably at the library," Daniel said, touching his matching necklace.

"Drumming!"

He pressed the down button. "Or reading. I hear some people do that in libraries."

"So how do you think we get can back to the island?" Joy asked as the elevator rose toward them with a *clank-clang-grrrr*.

"I guess we just have to wait," Daniel said.

"I can't stand waiting," Joy said, tapping the elevator doors.

Clank-clang-grrrr, the elevator said.

"Well, I can't stand you drumming on everything," Daniel said.

Clank-clang-boom, the elevator said.

Clank-boom-badoom.

Clang! Badoom-doom. Boom-ba-BOOM.

Joy squealed. "Do you hear that?"

Boom-badoom-doom-boom-ba-BOOM.

"It's happening again!" Daniel said.

BOOM-boom-BOOM! The rhythm thundered, louder and louder. *Boom-BADOOM-boom!*

When the elevator doors opened, brilliant sunlight streamed through.

Daniel saw a thousand bright-green leaves swaying in a brisk breeze. Then the drumbeat

whooshed him into the elevator and straight through the other side.

He heard Joy whooping nearby, then felt himself falling—down, down, down!

Chapter 2

Daniel landed as gently as a feather on a melted marshmallow—and the apartment building was gone.

Instead, he was standing in the branches of a tree. A massive tree, with a trunk thicker than a pickup truck. Afternoon sunlight glowed through slender leaves that sprouted in starburst patterns. Seedpods dangled from stems, and a warm breeze wafted through the branches of the forest all around, making the leaves rustle against each other.

Birds chirped, frogs croaked, and the air smelled

like water and flowers—and also like the terrarium that Ms. Park kept in her third-grade classroom.

"We did it!" Joy said, standing on the branch beside him. "We're here!"

"Where?" he asked, because he couldn't see anything except trees in every direction, some with daggerlike fronds, some dangling strands of moss.

"Here!" She hopped up and down on the branch. "On the biggest tree in the world."

"Stop that before you break the branch," Daniel said.

"It's too ginormous to break," she said, giving one last stomp.

Joy craned her neck to peer upward, and Daniel did the same. A few patches of blue sky peeked in between the thick layers of leaves, giving them a glimpse of colorful birds gliding through the air. A shiny green beetle crawled on a twig, and a little lizard chased a big lizard around a branch with spiky red flowers.

"That one's pretty," Daniel said, pointing at the flowers. "I bet Kimani will know what it is. She's a tree expert."

"Yeah, but she's not here."

"Not yet," Daniel said. "She will be."

"What if she wasn't drumming?" Joy gave a shiver of horror. "What if she was... studying?"

"She *was* studying," a faint voice called from above. "And she got zapped here anyway."

"There you are!" Daniel called back as he looked up.

Kimani stepped into view on a higher branch. She looked just the same, with bright eyes and a ponytail sort of like Joy's, except hers didn't have a chunky blue hair-tie. She wore a purple backpack, and her T-shirt said: *Worm Shmurm—I'm a Book DRAGON!*

"Ha!" Joy said to Daniel, before calling to Kimani. "He didn't believe me."

"What?" Kimani yelled.

"Daniel didn't believe we'd come back here," Joy shouted.

"What?" Kimani yelled again.

"Hold on!" Daniel bellowed to Kimani. "We're coming up!"

"Give me a lift," Joy told him.

He cupped his hands together and Joy stepped on his interwoven fingers, then scrambled easily up to Kimani's branch. She and Kimani hugged while they waited for Daniel to join them.

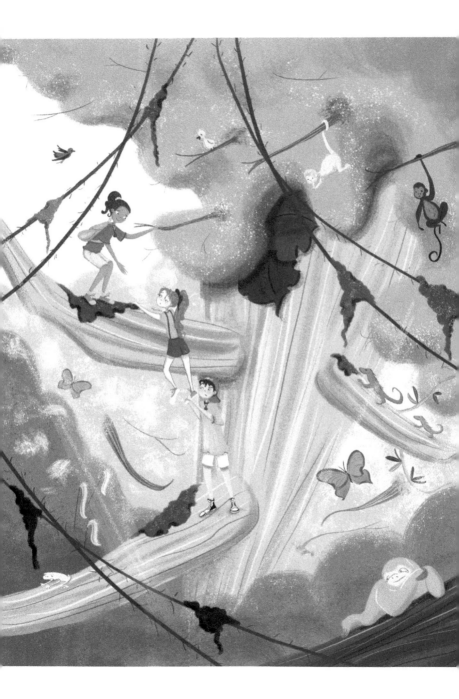

"C'mon, slow poke," Joy said.

Daniel hefted himself onto the next branch. Halfway up, he realized that it was a loooong way to the ground. They were so far up that he couldn't even *see* the ground, just the trunk disappearing into the leaves below him. He almost slid back to the safety of his original branch, but then Kimani offered her hand and helped him up.

He plopped down next to her, and the three of them dangled their legs from the higher branch.

"Here we are again," he said. "Stuck in the middle of nowhere without a clue."

"I know." Joy stretched out on her back on the branch. "Awesome, right?"

"Well..." Daniel looked at the endless sunlit leaves surrounding them. "Yeah, this is pretty awesome."

"And we do have one clue," Kimani said. "We know we're in a rainforest."

"How can you tell?" Daniel asked.

"The air is humid and tropical. You can smell the water—and hear birds singing and bugs buzzing and everything."

"See?" he told Joy. "Tree expert."

"Well, I'm not sure what kind of tree this is, but

we're definitely in the forest canopy," Kimani said. "That's where the treetops come together to form a giant leafy cover made of leaves, branches, and vines."

"What?" Daniel shouted.

"Like a hundred-foot-tall umbrella," Kimani said.

"I mean, what did you say? I can barely hear you over all the noise!"

"Oh, that's just the canopy animals buzzing and squawking," Kimani said.

"Sounds like the canopy is the busiest spot in the jungle," Joy said.

"For sure," Kimani agreed. "More animals live in the canopy than anywhere else in rainforest."

"I can see why they like it up here," Daniel said, leaning over to peer below them. "It's pretty dark down there..."

"That's the understory," Kimani said, pulling Daniel back upright. "And underneath that is the scariest story of all—the forest floor, where the most ferocious animals in the jungle live."

"Ooh, like what?" Joy asked, looking down eagerly.

"Like the giant hairy Brazilian Wandering Spider," Kimani said, "which has the deadliest venom of any spider in the world."

"I know about those," Joy said. "First they paralyze you so you can't move a muscle. Then your throat and lungs close up until—"

"Okaaaaaay," Daniel said. "I've heard enough about what's creeping around on the forest floor."

"But I didn't even get to tell you about the jaguar's skull-crushing bite," Kimani told him. "Or the enormous slithering ana—"

"Whoa, look at that!" Joy said, pointing toward the shady bottom of the canopy layer.

A dozen small shadowy figures darted from branch to branch, then leaped through the air. They climbed vines and sped through the dappled leaf-shadows like a mob of undersized acrobats.

And they didn't sound like birds, chirping and tweeting happily. Instead, they sounded like goblins, hooting and snarling and screaming—and they were racing closer!

Chapter 3

Daniel scrambled to his feet on the branch. "What are they?"

"I don't know—" Kimani started, just as one of the creatures leaped into sight above them. "Oh!"

The creature was small and furry with a long, skinny tail. Two black eyes peered from its fuzzy, white face, which had a gray patch covering the nose and mouth.

"Monkeys!" Joy laughed. "Too cute. And there's a whole entire pack of them!"

"A troop," Kimani said.

"Look how long their tails are," Daniel said. "They're like twice the length of their bodies."

"That's called a prehensile tail," Kimani explained. "It works like a fifth arm. The monkeys of the rainforest are the only monkeys in the world that have them. It helps them move through the canopy more easily and gives them a backup plan in case the other four arms accidentally miss a branch."

"That way they won't fall down on the dangerous forest floor," Joy said.

"Imagine how many baskets I could shoot with five arms," Daniel said.

"And look," Joy said, "some of those monkey arms have babies in them!"

Daniel spotted one with a baby and a handful of others calmly chomping on green-skinned fruit. But most of the monkeys were hooting and yowling and glaring.

"Um," he said. "They don't look happy."

"That one does," Joy said. "The little one on the branch."

Daniel followed her gaze and saw a baby monkey crawling along a narrow branch. It was heading toward a bunch of yellow butterflies with black-tipped wings that were flitting through the air.

And as the monkey crawled closer, the branch wobbled and shook in its little paws.

"It looks happy," he said. "But it doesn't look safe."

Joy scoffed. "It's a monkey. It knows how to climb trees."

"But it's only a baby—" Daniel started, and the

branch beneath the monkey bent down sharply.

"Oh," Joy said, her breath catching. "You're right.
It's going to fall!"

"Stop!" Daniel yelled at the baby. "Stop moving,
you dumb monkey!"

"Forget the butterflies!" Kimani called. "Come this
way, little monkey!"

The baby didn't even glance at them. It kept staring at the yellow butterflies flapping and fluttering. It crawled forward as the branch bent below it. Then it stretched out one little paw... and the branch snapped!

An instant before the baby tumbled from the treetops, a grown-up monkey reached out and snagged its arm, chattering sharply.

"Whew!" Joy said.

"That must be its mother," Kimani said.

"Strap your baby in a car seat!" Daniel shouted.

The other monkeys didn't like that. Some bared their teeth, some paced and made rude gestures, and the rest screamed and shook the tree branches so hard that twigs rained down on Daniel.

"What are they saying?" Joy asked Kimani.

"How should I know? I don't speak monkey."

"I think they want us to go away," Daniel said.

"Just like my sister," Joy said.

"Well, they're right about one thing." Daniel picked a twig out of his hair. "We can't just hang around in a tree all day."

"We need to find a poem that tells us what to do. Like last time," Joy said.

"I don't see any poems up here," Kimani said. "Let's go check on the forest floor."

"Are you bananas?" Daniel cried. "What about all those deadly spiders wandering around down there?"

Joy grinned. "Well, they *are* also called banana spiders."

"Just don't make any sudden moves on the way down," Kimani said. "We don't want to scare the monkeys."

"Tell *them* not to scare *me*," Daniel grumbled.

The monkeys' angry calls grew fainter as Daniel, Kimani, and Joy lowered themselves carefully from one branch to another. When they were most of the way to the forest floor, the tree's leaves thinned and the tops of saplings and smaller trees appeared around them.

As the sunlight dimmed, Kimani said, "Now this is the understory I was telling you about. Here, I'll show you how it works." She took out her notebook and flipped through the pages.

Daniel saw that Kimani had sketched pictures of the rocks and shipwreck from their last adventure on Sharktooth Island. She'd written down the words to the poems they'd found there too. When she got to a blank page, she began to sketch a whole mess of trees.

"We started in the canopy," she said as she drew.

"You mean the giant green umbrella that we've been crawling through this whole time," Joy said.

"Yep," Kimani said. "And now we've reached the understory, which grows in the shade of the higher trees."

"The understory trees look so tiny compared to the canopy trees," Daniel said, "but their leaves are humongous!"

"Their big leaves help them catch the few specks of sunlight that manage to sneak through the canopy," Kimani explained. "The speckled sunlight also makes the understory a perfect hiding spot for speckled animals... like ocelots."

"You mean those adorable spotted kitty cats?" Joy said. "Here, kitty, kitty!"

"Those adorable spotted kitty cats use their razor-sharp claws to tear their prey into bite-sized morsels."

"Wandering spiders *and* killer ocelots?" Daniel said, his eyes going wide.

"And under the understory is the forest floor," Kimani said, doodling a carpet of dead leaves at the bottom of the page.

"So the rainforest has three layers, like my sister's birthday cake," Joy said.

"Actually, it has four," Kimani said, continuing to doodle.

"Is the fourth layer made of broccoli?" Daniel asked.

"No," Kimani said.

"Then why are you drawing broccoli?"

"That's not broccoli, that's the overstory. It's made up of the tallest trees in the rainforest that pop out above the canopy."

"Are they broccoli trees?"

"Broccoli doesn't grow in... oh, never mind! Let's just keep climbing down. We're almost to the forest floor."

A hummingbird sipped from purple flowers that hung in clusters from a nearby tree, and a green-and-yellow frog with red eyes leaped away from Daniel as he climbed.

He smiled after the frog. Half of the animals and plants in the rainforest were as bright and colorful as cartoons. But when he climbed down farther, he stopped smiling.

Because the forest floor wasn't there.

Chapter 4

Daniel straddled a low branch. The rainforest
canopy blocked most of the sunlight, so everything
below was dim and shadowy. Still, he saw the tree's
roots curving outward, each one as wide as a park
bench, while orange-leafed shrubs and thick-stemmed
ferns rose between them.

But the roots didn't burrow into the forest floor—
they vanished into a swamp.

The water was so black that it looked like motor oil.
Tuffets of grass poked through the surface here and

there. Ripples spread when leaves and twigs fell from above, and spindly bugs skated across the surface.

"Can we wade through it?" Daniel asked.

"Let's see." Kimani climbed to the roots and dunked a long stick into the water until it disappeared. "Nope. Too deep. And I don't see helpful little poems on any of these trees."

"Me neither."

"We need a raft," Joy said, sliding down the trunk to another root.

"Where are we going to get a raft?" Daniel asked.

"We'll build one!" She clambered toward the other side of the tree. "Ooh, or a canoe!"

Daniel hopped down beside Kimani. "Can we do that?"

"How would I know?"

"You're a book dragon, you know everything."

"We might be able to build a raft," Kimani said, looking around. "If we spent hours and hours. And if we knew how."

"There are probably instructions in your notebook," Daniel told her.

"But there aren't."

"I bet there are."

"I think I'd remember if I'd written raft-building instructions in my—" She saw his teasing expression and slugged his arm. "Oh, shut your mouth."

"I found a path!" Joy shouted from the other side of the tree.

Daniel followed Kimani around the trunk and saw Joy standing in the middle of the swamp. Except no, she was standing on a root that stretched across the water.

Joy spread her arms like she was walking on a balance beam, then hopped to another root, a few feet away. That one curved through the water from the next tree over.

"We can run from tree to tree across these roots until the swamp ends," she yelled.

"Is that the right way?" Kimani called. "To lead us out of here?"

"Even better," Joy hollered back. "It's the *only* way!"

Kimani laughed, then she and Daniel followed the root to the neighboring tree in the shadow of the rainforest canopy. By the time they reached it, Joy was already returning to them along another root.

"This one's a dead end," she said. "It doesn't reach the roots of the next tree."

"It's like a labyrinth!" Kimani said.

"Or a maze," Joy said, jogging off. "C'mon, this way!"

Daniel and Kimani followed, balancing on the root to next tree, and then the one after that. The air smelled thick and mossy, and in a few places the swamp water was just inches beneath their sneakers.

Then Joy called from ahead. "There's nowhere else to go. We're going to have to swim."

Edging along the root toward her, Daniel glanced down at the swamp. He didn't love the idea of swimming through that black water. There were probably banana spiders or piranhas or crocodiles or—

He spotted a gleaming shape in the water. A long, smooth branch floated in the sluggish current. *Very* long, like a telephone pole. But it moved too quickly among the drowned ferns, disappearing down under the water, then popping up again.

"Um, guys?" he said as the branch moved toward them. "Is that a snake?"

"Nah," Joy said. "It's too big to be a snake."

Except when the branch rose from the water, it had a pointy face, black eyes, and a glistening body that slithered endlessly onto the roots of a nearby tree. It was huge. Thicker than any telephone pole, with greenish-brown scales and black spots that reminded Daniel of a leopard. And a forked tongue that flickered from its terrible mouth as it tasted the air.

"Not if it's an anaconda," Kimani whispered.

Chapter 5

"**B**-b-big," Daniel stammered, staring at the snake.

"So, *so* big," Joy said, her voice hushed for once.

"And beautiful," Kimani said.

Daniel might have thought that nothing in the world could've made him look away from the snake, but his head jerked toward Kimani. "*What?*"

"Look at her! She's gorgeous."

The anaconda's tongue flickered again. "O-kay," Daniel said. "Let's enjoy her gorgeousness from higher in this tree."

Joy scratched her cheek. "What about the monkeys?"

"They're gone," Daniel said. "And anyway, they're not as scary as a monster snake."

"Anacondas are completely misunderstood," Kimani said. "They only hunt when they're hungry."

"Maybe she's hungry now," Daniel said, boosting Joy onto a higher branch.

"And they almost never bother humans," Kimani continued.

"*Almost*?" Daniel asked.

"C'mon, Kimani!" Joy said, reaching down.

Kimani took her hand and scrambled onto the branch. "Plus, there's never been a proven case of an anaconda eating a human."

"*Proven*?" Daniel asked, as Kimani helped him up.

"Would you stop repeating everything I say? Snakes are cool. I love them."

"I like them too," Daniel told her. "Behind glass, in a zoo."

Joy gave a shiver. "I don't even like them then."

"I thought you weren't scared of anything," Kimani said to her.

"I'm not! Except snakes. And blueberries."

"Blueberries?"

"Long story," Daniel told Kimani.

"They're so squishy on the inside," Joy explained with another shiver.

"Uh, that's the shortest story ever," Kimani said as she looked down at the anaconda.

Daniel followed Kimani's gaze. "And that's the longest snake."

"Is it poisonous?" Joy asked.

"Venomous," Kimani said. "But no."

Joy frowned at Kimani. "What? It *is* venomous, but it's not?"

"Oh! No, it's just that poisonous and venomous mean different things. Poisonous means you shouldn't bite it. Venomous means it shouldn't bite you."

"So which is it, Kimani?" Daniel asked, because she still hadn't told them if the snake was venomous or poisonous—or just big enough to chomp them in half.

"Neither! Anacondas are constrictors, like boas. They don't poison their prey, they just wrap them up in their school bus–sized bodies and give them a nice, tight..." Kimani noticed the fear in her friends' eyes. "A nice, tight hug!"

"W-what kinds of animals do they like to hug most?" Joy asked, showing very un-Joy-like nerves.

"Oh, you know, fish, turtles, pigs, crocodiles, and pretty much any animal the size of a small deer."

"*I'm* the size of a small deer," Joy said faintly.

"Maybe keep some facts to yourself," Daniel told Kimani, even though he was kind of fascinated.

"Sorry," Kimani said.

Daniel eyed the swamp warily. "So, we climb the tree... and then what?"

"That's obvious," Joy said as she shook her head and grinned. "We copy the monkeys!"

"You want to leap from branch to branch?" he asked.

"Only more than anything," she said. "Don't you?"

He stared at her. "No, Joy."

"Why not?"

"Because I'm not a monkey! I don't have one of those fancy arm tails to make sure I don't do a hundred-foot freefall through the rainforest."

"You're right about climbing though," Kimani told him. "Once we get to the overstory, we can look across the treetops and find out where we are."

"And we'll be farther from the snake," Daniel said.

The branches were too far apart for easy climbing, so Kimani developed a system: first Daniel would give Joy a boost to a higher branch, then Joy would help

Kimani up, and finally Kimani would help Daniel.

"How far up is the overstory again?" Joy asked, pulling herself up to the next branch.

"Only two hundred feet," Kimani said. "Easy peasy when we work together. Plus, the sightseeing is amazing."

As they climbed, more sunlight filtered through the trees. When Kimani stopped to open her notebook and sketch a line of ants marching along a branch, Daniel wondered if that one tree was the ants' entire world. Then Joy paused to pick white fluff from a seedpod while Daniel gazed toward the sound of birdsong. He hoped that DaVinci—the chatty parrot they'd met on their last adventure—would swoop onto his shoulder.

The bird calls slowly faded, though, without any parrot flying toward him.

Daniel lifted Joy to the next branch... and she laughed in surprise. "Look!" she said.

"All I can see is your sneaker in my face," he said.

"Well, come up here and *then* look!" she said, wriggling to the top of the branch.

"You can go next," Kimani offered Daniel.

"That's okay," he said. "We've got a good system,

let's stick with it."

She shot him a teasing smile. "That's kind of your thing, huh?" she said.

"You know the saying," he answered. "'If it ain't broke...'"

A thumping sounded above them, like Joy was kicking something.

"...wait four seconds, and Joy will break it," Kimani finished.

"I heard that!" Joy said, popping over the side to help Kimani up.

When Daniel joined them, he saw what Joy had been talking about: the next branch wasn't just a branch, it was a *floor*. A wooden platform of warped planks—scattered with leaves and twigs and bird poop—wrapped around the trunk of the tree.

Chapter 6

"**W**hat is this?" Daniel asked.

"It reminds me of the shipwreck on Sharktooth Island," Kimani said.

"Yeah," Joy said. "There are even bits of sail and rope and stuff."

Kimani looked around. "No poem though."

"There's something even better." Joy trotted to the edge of the platform, ducking under some low-hanging leaves. "Look!"

Daniel followed more slowly. Sure, the platform

felt solid, but they were a hundred and fifty feet above the ground. At least. He slipped carefully around the dangling leaves... and gasped at the sight in front of him.

The treetops spread below them like rolling hills. Sunlight gleamed on leaves that rippled in the breeze. Small colorful birds quickly darted through the branches, while bigger birds rode the wind in the blue, cloudless sky. In the distance, the rainforest ended

and waves glinted around dozens of islands in the endless ocean.

"I guess we reached the overstory," Kimani said, stepping beside him. "This tree is higher than the rest."

"We're back on Sharktooth Island!" Joy spread her arms. "Look, there's the beach and the shipwreck."

"Uh..." Daniel stared at a cloud of black smoke rising from a mountainous island. "Is that a volcano?"

"Looks like," Kimani said.

"Let's not go *that* way."

"We'll head there." Joy pointed to a spot on their own island. "See that little mountain?"

A pointy hill rose from the fields and meadows that started where the rainforest ended. Grass covered most of the hillside. White boulders were scattered here and there, and an even pointier shape, like a branchless tree, lofted high from one side of the hill. Except it didn't really look like a tree. It looked more like...

"Is that a tower?" Daniel asked, squinting.

"Only the coolest tower in the world," Joy said.

A line of windows spiraled up the outside wall of the round stone tower. Flower gardens with crumbling arches and overgrown hedges surrounded it, then stopped when the hillside dropped off steeply, falling toward the grassland.

"I wonder if it's part of a castle," Kimani said.

"That's where we're going," Joy announced.

"Why?" Daniel asked.

"Because whoever crashed their ship on the beach lives in that tower. Obviously!"

"How is that obvious?" Daniel asked.

"Plus," Joy told him, "Kimani says it's definitely part of a mysterious ruined castle."

Kimani tugged her ponytail. "Um, I said it might be."

"Exactly! And check out the roof. It has the same decorations as the treasure chest we found."

"You're right!" Kimani said, shading her eyes to look closer. "The star pattern!"

When Daniel spotted the familiar circle filled with stars on the tower, he felt a jolt of excitement. That's where they'd find a new poem. Or maybe even where they'd finally meet the mysterious drummer who'd magically summoned them to the island.

"We should get moving," Kimani said.

"Yeah," Joy said. "We don't want to make the queen wait."

"What queen?" Daniel asked.

"The *queen* queen! Who else lives in a castle?"

Kimani told Joy, "I meant, we should get moving because we don't want to get stuck in the forest at sundown."

"Oh," Joy said. "That too."

"Yeah," Daniel said. "That's when the nocturnal predators come out."

He was hoping Joy would ask what "nocturnal" meant so he could show Kimani that he knew some facts too, but she didn't.

"And the sun's already getting lower," Kimani said.

Daniel wrinkled his nose. "How do we reach the tower with that sea serpent beneath us?"

"We must've missed a clue," Kimani said. "Let's look again. Maybe we'll find a message."

"Or some of that green fruit," Daniel said. "I'm hungry."

"The monkey fruit?"

"It looked tasty."

Kimani made a face. "No way."

"Way!" a voice called.

Daniel spun toward the voice. "DaVinci?"

"Ahoy!" A turquoise-and-yellow blur of feathers swooped past. "Matey!"

"DaVinci!" Daniel sang out. "Over here!"

The parrot circled Joy. "Pretty! Pretty!"

"You're pretty too!" Joy told him.

With a gust of wind, DaVinci landed on Daniel's shoulder. His sharp claws dug through Daniel's shirt, but Daniel didn't mind.

"Long time no see," Kimani said, rubbing DaVinci's

chest feathers with one finger.

"Way!" DaVinci said.

"Where did you come from?" Daniel asked the parrot.

DaVinci spread his wings. "Crow's nest!"

"Silly bird! You're not a crow."

"That's not what he means," Kimani said. "A crow's nest is also what you call a lookout spot at the very top of a ship's mast."

"At the *very* top?" Daniel looked upward, peering through the fluttering layers of leaves. "I wonder..."

"That's it!" Kimani pointed above them. "Look, there's another platform even higher in the tree!"

"That must be where our message is," Daniel said.

"Only one way to find out," Kimani said.

Chapter 7

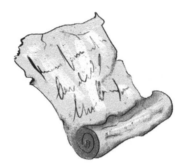

Daniel liked climbing trees while the forest surrounded him, but this tree wasn't tucked safely in the forest. It stood alone, towering above the rest. Which made him feel a little shaky.

Still, he followed the bobbing of Joy's red braid—and her chunky blue hair tie—upward until he reached the next platform. As he scrambled over the last branch, he felt DaVinci grip his shirt more tightly.

Kimani crept a little too close to the edge of the platform and peered across the canopy, and at first

Daniel thought she was trying to identify the trees or spot more "beautiful" snakes.

"The sun's still high, but it's heading down," Kimani said.

"We're running out of time," Daniel said.

"Not a problem!" Joy called from the other end of the platform.

Daniel tested the strength of the boards, then walked toward his cousin. "What did you find?"

"Only *this*." She turned toward him, brandishing a torn scrap of parchment. "I found the poem!"

"Whoa," Daniel said.

"Avast!" DaVinci said, launching from Daniel's shoulder.

"Totally avast," Joy agreed, as the parrot's colorful blur soared around them.

"What's it say?" Daniel asked.

"Wait, wait!" Kimani rummaged in her backpack for her pen and notebook. "Okay, now."

Joy cleared her throat and read aloud:

Fly through the forest, without any wings.
Hurry! Don't linger or stall!
Get to my tower before the night brings
Shadows and shivers and falls.

"You were right about getting there before sundown," Joy told Kimani, who was writing the poem in her notebook.

"Of course she was right," Daniel said. "But how do we fly without wings?"

"Um..." Joy squinted as she thought. "With propellers? Or a catapult!"

"We're not building another catapult."

"We should—" Kimani looked up from her notebook. "Wait... *another* catapult?"

Daniel nodded. "Yeah, Joy built one with a frying pan and baby stroller. She launched our old stuffed animals from the twenty-third-floor window."

"*We* built one and launched stuffed animals," Joy reminded him.

"We didn't mean to hit the playground..." Daniel sighed. "They sort of burst. There was stuffing everywhere."

Kimani laughed. "You two are so weird."

"You're the one who calls monster snakes 'beautiful,'" Daniel reminded her.

"Anacondas aren't monsters." Kimani tucked her notebook into her backpack. "And they *are* beautiful! But I'm not sure how we fly without wings if we do the catapult."

"Yeah." Joy sighed "I guess we'll have to use the tightrope."

Daniel blinked at her. "The what now?"

"You know." Joy pointed toward the tree trunk. "The tightrope. Right there."

Daniel squinted at the swaying leaves and vines. "I don't see—oh!"

A black rope looped the trunk above their heads, then stretched out, away from the tree, and disappeared downward into the canopy. Daniel had thought it was a vine, but now that he looked closer, he didn't know how he'd missed it.

"Cool," he said. "And look! It's slanting down to a platform on another tree."

"Except we're not tightrope walkers." When Kimani examined the rope, something caught her eye. "Hey, look! There's stuff tucked here between the boards and the branches."

"What kind of stuff?" Joy asked.

"Belts and straps and cords." Kimani pulled them out one by one, before holding up smooth length of wood. "And driftwood."

"What's driftwood doing here?" Daniel asked.

"Same thing as the tightrope!" Joy said. "It's waiting for us."

"Hard to port!" DaVinci squawked.

"Here's some rope that looks like the rigging from a ship," Kimani said.

Joy wrinkled her nose. "What're we supposed to do with all of this?"

"And where did it come from?" Daniel wondered aloud. "Who tied the tightrope in place?"

"The mysterious drummer," Joy guessed. "But how did he know we'd climb this tree?"

"He sent DaVinci to tell us about the crow's nest," Daniel told her.

"Pretty!" DaVinci said, landing beside Kimani.

"Thank you," Kimani said as she sketched in her notebook.

"What're you drawing?" Daniel asked her.

Kimani's hand moved quickly across the page. "Ziplines! That's what it is, not a tightrope. That's what the poem means. Instead of walking on it, we'll swing on the zipline across the canopy!"

She turned her notebook toward him. The picture she drew showed a stick figure holding onto a belt looped around the tightrope—or zipline—then sliding down toward the next tree on the other end of the rope.

"See how the rope is angled downward?" Kimani pointed with her pencil. "That's how I knew it was a zipline and not a tightrope. Ziplines only work if they are at the right slope."

"You mean how it's slanted?" Daniel asked.

"Yeah. A zipline needs to be at a steep enough slope so that gravity pulls you along, but not so steep that you go too fast and crash at the other end."

"Looks awesome!" Joy said.

"Looks dangerous," Daniel muttered.

Chapter 8

"**H**ow can we tell if the angle is too steep?" Daniel asked.

"I don't know," Kimani said. "I don't *think* it's too steep."

Daniel made a face. "We need some helmets and harnesses."

"Like a monkey needs a car seat?" Joy teased.

"Yes!" Daniel said.

"Well, we don't have any."

"What if we make seats from the driftwood?"

Kimani asked. "We can loop cords around the zipline, one cord for each of us. Then Joy can tie the ends of the cords to the driftwood. We can hold onto the cords, sit on the driftwood, and... *zoom*."

"Zoom is good," Joy said. "I love zoom."

Kimani looked at Daniel. "Does that sound okay?"

"I guess, as long as we test if it's safe first. We can use something heavy to make sure it works."

"You're heavy," Joy told him.

"We're not testing it on me!" Daniel said.

Except they were.

Kimani sorted the cords and rope according to thickness and texture. Then she picked up a bristly length of cord. "This one seems strong."

Daniel ran his fingers along the cord, which felt as rough as sandpaper. He looked at Joy. "Make sure the knots are strong too."

"I will," she said. "I promise."

She sounded serious for once, which was a relief. This wasn't just launching stuffed animals from the window; this was launching *themselves* out over the jungle a hundred feet below. Daniel didn't want his own personal stuffing to burst everywhere.

Kimani looped a cord around the zipline while

Daniel snapped the driftwood into three pieces. Joy knotted the cord's loop into place, then tied the bottom of the dangling cord to the middle of one of the driftwood pieces.

"Okay, Daniel," Kimani said. "Wait until Joy and I get into position, then sit on the driftwood and lift your feet, and let's see what happens."

"Into position?" he asked.

"At the end of the platform. So Joy and I could, um..."

"Catch you if the knot unravels and you're about to tumble to your doom," Joy said, trotting to the farthest edge of the platform.

"Great," Daniel muttered.

Nervously, he held the cord and straddled the driftwood. He had to stand on his tiptoes because the tree trunk was so close behind him that the zipline made his seat high. He lowered down slowly until he was standing flat-footed, the driftwood pulled up tight against him. The zipline barely sagged, tied firmly to the trees on both ends and stretched tight.

"Well, it holds my weight and the knot's still tight," Daniel said. "I guess we've done everything right so far..."

"We make a good team," Kimani said.

Daniel bounced on his toes a few times. The driftwood felt okay under his butt. Strong and steady. His hands already ached from holding the cord tight.

"Oh," Joy told Kimani. "That reminds me..."

Daniel took a breath. He started to sit with his full weight on the driftwood when—

"Wait!" Joy shouted. "Hold on!"

He stopped, his heart pounding. "What? What's wrong?"

"Kimani said we make a good team," Joy told him.

"I heard!"

"And good teams," she continued, "wear team colors!"

She unwound her hair from the bulky hair tie, then unbraided the strands until she was holding three blue loops that had been woven together. Three blue *headbands*.

Daniel stared at her. "You wore that every day for weeks just for this moment, didn't you?"

"Of course!" Joy said, handing one to Kimani before running over to give one to Daniel.

Kimani tugged the headband into place. "Fits perfectly."

"We rule," Joy said, finger-combing her ponytail out before wearing her headband.

Daniel wasn't so sure about the headband, but Kimani and Joy looked happy, so he tugged his down over his head.

"Pretty!" DaVinci squawked.

"Thanks," Daniel said.

"Pretty, but *slow*," Joy said, returning to the end of the platform. "C'mon, Daniel, start zooming!"

"Here I go," he said, but he didn't. He just stood there, waiting for the right moment, like when he was playing basketball and suddenly knew that *this* was time to take the shot.

"C'mon!" Joy called.

"Give him a second," Kimani told her.

"We need to reach the castle before sunset."

"I know, but—"

"Yeeeeee-haw!" Daniel yelled, shouting extra loudly to give himself courage. "Gravity take me away!"

And he lifted his feet from the platform.

Chapter 9

With all of Daniel's weight on the driftwood, he should've started sliding down the angled zipline, past the girls, then into the air between the trees. He should've flashed through the canopy, speeding downward until he reached the platform at the next tree.

Instead, he just dangled there.

Exactly where he'd started.

"More zipping," Joy called. "Less swaying."

"Walk the plank!" DaVinci squawked, landing on Daniel's shoulder.

"I'm trying to." Daniel kicked his feet like he was on a swing, but he still didn't go anywhere. "Stupid gravity."

"Stop messing around," Joy said, while Kimani toyed with the bead on her necklace, lost in thought.

"I'm not messing!" he told Joy. "I'm just not moving."

"Then *start* messing," she said.

"The rope's stuck on the zipline." He kicked his feet again. "It's not sliding."

"Why not?"

"How should I know? Maybe it's not steep enough."

"Friction!" Kimani announced.

"Huh?" Daniel said.

Kimani came closer to examine the cord. "That cord is too rough."

"But it's the strongest one," he said as he got off the driftwood seat.

"We need a smoother cord. Otherwise, the friction will keep making it hard for you to move anywhere."

"Stupid friction" Daniel said. "Go find someone else to pick on."

"Friction is not picking on you, Daniel," Kimani giggled. "Friction is everywhere. It's just doing its thing: creating resistance between surfaces."

"You sound like my science teacher," Joy said. "Only your socks match."

"That's because it *is* science. And once you understand how science works, you can figure out how to work with it!"

Kimani pulled out the bits of rope and straps that she had tucked in her backpack. One strap was coated with tar, which was weird. "Hmm," Kimani said, running here fingers over the sticky strap. "This one's not gonna work."

She rubbed the next bit of rope. "This one seems pretty strong. And slippery enough. A definite maybe."

Daniel tried pushing forward again from his seat on the driftwood. But he didn't budge. Not even an inch.

"Have you ever tried going down a dry waterslide?" Kimani asked, rubbing the next piece of rope. "You can't because there's too much friction. But when you add water to the mix, it reduces the friction and then you slide down as fast and easily as a greased watermelon."

"So we should grease Daniel like a watermelon?" Joy asked.

"Or do I need to sit on this driftwood until it rains?" Daniel asked.

"Good thing we are in the *rain*forest," Joy said.

"No," Kimani said. "Let's try another one. Think about the smooth metal slide at the playground. It's easy to slide down because there is very little friction between your jeans and the metal. But what if the slide was made of carpet instead?"

"Ouch, carpet burn," Joy said.

"Right," Kimani said. "The carpet creates friction and your jeans create friction, so when you rub the two together you've got way too much resistance to slide anywhere. The same thing is happening to Daniel right now. The zipline is rough and the cord looped around it is rough. So..."

"So I'm going nowhere fast down a carpet slide!" Daniel said.

"I've got it!" Joy said. "We should find a smoother cord to loop around the zipline."

"Exactly!" Kimani said, untying the knots on the rough cord.

DaVinci squawked encouragement as the kids examined the different cords and straps and discussed which would be the best one for job.

The treetops were still bright with daylight, but Daniel didn't know how much longer they had before

sunset. And Kimani kept glancing toward the horizon, looking more and more worried as Joy tied a new cord—one that felt as smooth as glass—around the zipline.

Then the girls got back into position and Daniel stood on his tiptoes, straddling the driftwood.

"Maybe this time," he started, and jumped forward, tucking his feet below him. "I'll actually—"

His breath caught as he shot along the platform then sped through the canopy. Far, far above the ground.

Chapter 10

"**Y**aaaaaaa!" Daniel yelled, his heart pounding.

The wind whipped through his hair as he zipped downward. His seat twirled wildly and he saw a glimpse of the girls, then of the forest, then of the platform in the tree he was speeding toward.

Then he saw a parrot flying beside him, weaving effortlessly through the branches.

"Way!" DaVinci squawked.

"Show-off!" Daniel laughed, dizzy with exhilaration.

The branches blurred until his feet clunked

against the platform. He slid five or ten feet, his legs jouncing along, then ended up on his butt.

"Are you okay?" Kimani called from the other tree. "Daniel?"

"Was it awesome?" Joy called. " 'Cause it looked awesome!"

Daniel stood shakily and yelled, "It's *beyond* awesome!"

"I knew it! Hold on, we're coming!"

"Check your knots!" Daniel said, in case she'd forgotten.

"Kimani's next!" Joy called. "But she's a little scared."

"I was a lot scared," Daniel yelled back. "You'll love it, I promise."

"Okay," Kimani said. "Here I come."

But nothing happened. Joy said, "She's not moving!"

"I'm moving, I'm moving!" Kimani said. "I just need you to count. I'll go on three."

So together, Daniel and Joy called, "One, two..."

"*Three!*" Kimani yelled and leaped off the platform.

"Avast!" DaVinci flapped off to join her. "Walk the plank!"

Kimani screamed... and a second later, Daniel saw

her hurtling through the trees, her blue headband bright among the leaves. She was shrieking and laughing at the same time, and her eyes were shining with excitement.

She swooped down, her sneakers dragging on the boards. Daniel caught her arm as she landed, so she didn't end up on her butt.

"You were right!" She gave Daniel a quick hug. "That was amazing."

"I know, right?"

"C'mon, Joy!" she called, turning. "You're going to love—"

"*Aaaah-ah-oh-aa-ah!*" Joy cried like Tarzan, whipping toward them.

She hadn't waited for Kimani to land before jumping. She was already at the platform! Daniel leaped aside, but not quickly enough: Joy knocked him back onto his butt, then landed on his belly.

"Oof!" he said, though she was so small that it didn't really hurt.

"Sorry," she said.

"There's more stuff on this platform," Kimani said as she stepped closer to the tree's trunk. "Seashells, a few rocks and... yuck, a dirty old shirt."

"What good is that?" Daniel asked, rubbing his arm where he'd fallen.

"No clue. It's like the mysterious drummer left random stuff in case we needed it. We should take it with us." She unzipped her backpack and put in the items.

"If he knew Joy was coming," Daniel said, "he should've left elbow pads."

"There's another zipline over here," Joy called,

from the other side of the trunk. "Maybe we can zoom all the way across the forest!"

Daniel nodded. "Flying without wings."

"Let's untie the knots from our cords," Kimani said, "so Joy can attach our seats to the next zipline."

"Yeah, we can't linger or stall," Daniel said, quoting the poem. "We need to get to the tower before sunset."

Joy tied their cords and driftwood pieces to the new zipline. They zipped through the air again and landed on the next platform, where they found another zipline which they took to the next platform.

Each new platform had weird stuff on it—mostly stuff that seemed to be from shipwrecks, but also things like rusty bolts and a single flip-flop. Daniel wondered if the mysterious drummer had a plan or was just giving them random odds and ends.

Though he didn't wonder for long.

Instead, he zoomed past lizards and flowers and more brightly colored birds than he'd ever dreamed of. The forest canopy felt endless, like a whole planet of branches and leaves, fluttering in the sea breeze.

But the swamp felt endless too.

Every time Daniel glanced downward, he caught a glint of the setting sun against the black water. He wondered where the anaconda was. Hopefully still back at that first tree, dreaming about chomping on headband-wearing kids. Too bad for her! Daniel was high in the sky now, whooshing through the air with a happy parrot on his shoulder.

"We did it," Joy shouted as she landed on another platform. "We're almost through the forest!"

"With time to spare," Daniel said, looking toward the sun hanging just above the distant volcanic island.

"Well, a *little* time."

Joy brushed aside a cluster of leaves that were almost as big as she was. "I can see the castle."

"We'll get there soon," Kimani said. "Only two more trees. We're at the bottom of the canopy now. We'll zip through the understory and reach the forest floor."

"You mean the swamp," Daniel said.

"No, the swamp ends at the second tree up ahead," Kimani said, peering around some low-hanging leaves.

"So two more zips and then we hike to the castle," Daniel said.

"Without shadows or shivers or falls," Kimani said.

Joy gasped. "Oh no!"

"What's wrong?" Kimani asked.

"She *likes* shadows and shivers and falls," Daniel said.

"No, look!" Joy pointed downward. "A baby monkey is trapped in the swamp!"

Chapter 11

When Daniel looked over the edge of the platform, he spotted a little monkey stranded on the roots of the tree below him. A tiny monkey. A wide-eyed, fuzz-headed monkey, stumbling around unsteadily like a furry toddler.

"That's the same baby as before," Joy said.

"The dumb one," Daniel said.

"It must've fallen," Kimani said.

Daniel chewed his lower lip. "Where's its mother?"

"There!" Joy pointed at the troop of monkeys

leaping through the forest. "Look, the grown-ups are already coming."

"Thank goodness," Kimani said.

The grown-up monkeys suddenly stopped a few trees away. One started shrieking, and a second later they were all growling and snarling.

"They sound scared," Kimani said.

"Of us?" Daniel asked. "We're, like, fifty feet away."

Joy frowned. "Maybe they're worried the baby will slip into the swamp or—"

"The anaconda!" Kimani said.

A moment later, Daniel spotted a ripple in the black swamp water heading toward them. It looked slow and lazy, but was getting closer to the baby monkey.

Daniel swallowed. "Don't worry. The grown-up monkeys will save it."

They didn't though. The monkeys were too scared of the anaconda. They just shrieked louder, piercing cries that were echoed by what sounded like a thousand birds.

"I guess that's an alarm call," Kimani said above the din. "They're warning other monkeys."

"What about the little one?" Joy sounded like she

was going to cry. "What are we going to do?"

"Can we climb down and get it?" Daniel asked.

Kimani shook her head. "These branches are too far apart."

"Well, what do we have to work with?" he asked, looking around the platform.

"More driftwood." Kimani rummaged through a pile of stuff jammed between the platform and the tree trunk. "Broken pottery and a bunch of sea glass."

"Great," Daniel said. "That's a big help, mysterious drummer."

"There's a few vines past these huge leaves." Joy reached for a ropy shape dangling down from above. "Ew! Slimy."

Daniel spun toward her. "Are you sure that's not another snake?"

"Snakes aren't slimy," Kimani said.

"Of course I'm sure!" Joy said, prodding the vine again. "Uh, but where *is* the snake?"

"Still in the water," Kimani said. "She hasn't spotted the baby yet."

"Maybe she won't," Joy said.

"Maybe," Kimani said, but she didn't sound like she believed it.

"Oh!" Daniel said, eyeing a cluster of green fruit that hung over the platform from a neighboring tree. "There's fruit!"

"I don't care how hungry you are," Joy snapped at him. "We're not eating, we're saving the baby!"

"I'm not—"

"*And* you ate an entire pizza before we got here."

"I only had four slices," he said. "But that's not what I'm talking about."

"That's the same fruit the monkeys were eating earlier," Kimani said as she tugged her ponytail thoughtfully. "I know what you're thinking, Daniel! That's pretty smart."

He ducked his head. "Thanks."

"So, what are you thinking?" Joy asked him.

"We'll pelt the snake." He mimed throwing fruit at the swamp, toward the anaconda ripples that were spreading between the roots. "Maybe that'll scare her off."

"Uh," Kimani said, "that's not what I thought you were thinking."

"Ha!" Joy laughed. "Not so smart after all."

"No, no," Kimani said. "I just thought we could use the fruit as bait. We'll lower it somehow, then snag the baby and pull it up to safety."

"Monkey fishing," Joy said.

"Yeah," Daniel said. "That's better than snake pelting."

"But how do we snag the monkey?" Kimani asked.

"With a lasso," Joy told her. "Made out of vine!"

Daniel shook his head. "We're not going to lasso the monkey."

"I lassoed the lamp in my living room," she reminded him.

"But you were aiming for the chair."

"That's true. Um..." Joy tapped one of the big leaves beside her as she thought. "Oh! Let's make a basket from one of these huge leaves."

Kimani smiled. "That's perfect."

"It is?" Joy asked.

"It is!" Kimani said.

Daniel and Joy picked among the big leaves until they found a tough, leathery one with thick ribs running from the central stem. Kimani poked holes in the edges of the leaf with a bit of the sharp pottery, then Daniel got his fingers slimy as he snapped a vine loose from the branches above.

"Yuck," he said.

"I wonder if that goopy stuff is slime mold," Kimani said.

"Double-yuck," he said quickly before she could explain what "slime mold" was.

Joy wrinkled her nose at the gross vine. She poked one end through the holes Kimani made, like she was threading laces into a sneaker. She messed around with the leaf until the shape looked okay, then she tied a knot.

"It's not really a basket," Kimani said, looking at the loosely folded leaf.

"It's more like a swing," Daniel said. "A monkey swing."

Chapter 12

"**N**ow we just need bait," Joy said, carrying an armload of fruit over. "This actually smells pretty good."

"And I'm actually a little hungry," Daniel said, reaching for a ripe green fruit.

Kimani smacked his hand away. "That's monkey bait!"

"We don't need all of it."

"We might," Joy said.

"I should've had a fifth slice of pizza," he muttered.

Kimani snorted. "Hush up and grab the vine."

Daniel wrapped the slimy vine around one wrist like he was the anchor in a game of tug-of-war, while Kimani took hold of the middle. Once they were ready, Joy lowered the monkey swing over the side.

Even though the fruit didn't weigh much, the vine began slithering across Daniel's wrist and through his fingers.

"So slippery!" he said, tightening his grip.

"The slime is reducing the friction," Kimani told him. "That's why it's hard to hold."

"In other words, slime is slimy?"

"Ha. Yeah, I guess."

Joy looked over the edge while Daniel and Kimani lowered the monkey swing. "Good, keep going. Oh, the anaconda's leaving! No, now she's turning back. Wait, watch out!"

Daniel tightened his grip on the vine. "What's wrong?"

"You almost knocked the swing into the baby monkey!"

"Sorry, baby monkey!" Kimani called.

"Okay, now down the rest of the way," Joy said.

After the swing touched the roots of the tree,

Daniel trotted across the platform to see what was happening. The baby monkey didn't run away from a strange leaf-swing lowering from the sky. Instead, it peered at the curled shape curiously and crawled closer.

For a second, Daniel thought the baby was going to climb in. But then it looked at a shiny beetle just as curiously and started toward that. Halfway there, a bright patch of moss caught its eye. The baby sat on its furry little butt and peered at the moss.

"Why isn't it getting in?" Joy demanded. "Doesn't it know we're trying to save it?"

"C'mon, you dumb monkey," Daniel said, tugging on the vine to jostle the swing. "Pay attention to the pretty swing, not the boring moss!"

But the baby kept watching the moss. Meanwhile, the sun fell closer and closer to the horizon and the anaconda swam closer and closer to the monkey.

"We should've smooshed the fruit," Kimani said, fiddling with her headband. "To make the smell stronger."

"And easier to eat," Joy said. "Like baby food. Bring it back up, Daniel."

Daniel made a face, but he started pulling the

slimy vine. The first few feet were easy, then his hands started to cramp. It was hard to hold onto something so slippery!

"Help me out," he said.

Once Kimani and Joy pitched in, the vine slid quickly along the edge of the platform. The swing soared upward. A minute later, Joy dragged it onto the platform, careful not to lose the fruit inside.

"That's going to be harder with a monkey inside," Daniel said, wiping his palms on his pants.

"Yeah, we'll need to keep it totally steady," Kimani said. "Or the baby might fall."

Joy gasped. "Look at the anaconda."

The huge snake was slithering across the roots of a nearby tree. One that was way too close to the monkey. The snake kept stopping and tasting the air with its tongue too, like it knew the monkey was *somewhere*.

"If we don't act fast," Daniel said, "that monkey is going to be snake food."

DaVinci flashed down from above, and a clattering noise sounded across the platform. When Daniel turned, he realized that DaVinci must've been holding stuff in his beak: the platform was scattered with

striped leaves and yellow flowers, a cluster of berries, and a seedpod with white fluff. There were even a few of DaVinci's bluest feathers.

"You're just like the drummer," Daniel told the parrot. "What is all this useless stuff?"

"Pretty!" DaVinci squawked.

"I guess," Daniel said. "But what we need is..."

He trailed off when a sweet, fruity perfume filled the air. It was the most mouthwatering scent ever, and he was suddenly starving.

"That's better," Kimani said, smooshing the green fruits in the swing.

"Smells like tropical candy," he said. "Yum."

"Go away!" she told him. "It's still monkey bait!"

"Delicious, delicious monkey bait. Here, add the berries that DaVinci dropped."

"For all we know, they're poisonous."

"Or venomous," Joy said. "If *they* bite *you*."

"Very funny." He sighed. "I hope there really is a feast at the tower."

Kimani looked toward the setting sun. "If we don't leave now, we might never find out. We're running out of time."

Chapter 13

"**B**ut if we leave now," Joy said, "the snake will eat the monkey."

"So we can't leave." Kimani glanced at Daniel. "Right?"

He sighed. "Yeah. We need to help the fuzz-brained monkey."

"So we'll save the baby fast," Joy said. "Then zip off to the tower."

Daniel grabbed the vine. "Sounds good. Everyone ready?" He could feel the vine slowly slipping across his wrist again, so he looped it around his hand to tighten his grip.

"Ready!" Joy said as the vine slowly slipped through her fingers too.

"I don't think this is going to work," Kimani said, tugging her ponytail thoughtfully. "Once the weight of the monkey is added to the swing, it will be impossible for us to get a good enough grip on the slimy vine to pull him up. We need to build a pulley to do the work for us."

Joy fiddled with blue feathers that DaVinci had brought. "A pulley?"

"Yes. It's a simple machine that uses a rope and a counterweight to make it easier for people to move things to a higher place."

"Simple for you, maybe," Daniel said.

"A counter-*what?*" Joy asked.

"A counterweight. And we need to make one fast." Kimani picked another giant leaf and tied it to the other end of the vine to making a second swing.

"Are we rescuing two monkeys now?" Joy asked.

"No," Kimani said. "This swing will hold the counterweight."

She draped the vine across the platform and

dropped the new swing off the edge. It dangled exactly like the baby swing did, only on the opposite side of the platform.

"This reminds me of the balance scale in my science classroom," Joy said. "When you put a weight on one side, it sinks down. But when you add a heavier weight to the other side, it rises back up."

"Exactly!" Kimani said. "First, we'll lower the baby swing down to the ground. Then, as soon as the monkey crawls onto its swing, we'll put the counterweight in the other swing and lower that. As long as the counterweight is heavier, it will sink and baby monkey will rise."

"It'll totally work," Daniel said.

"I hope so," Joy said. "But how can we be sure the baby monkey climbs inside the swing?"

"That's what the smooshed fruit is for," he said.

"But what if it's not enough!" Joy said. "That baby monkey got distracted by a clump of moss. Do you think smooshed fruit has enough wow factor?"

"Well, if you have a pizza in your pocket—"

"We should decorate the swing!" Joy said. She showed him a blue parrot feather. "With the stuff DaVinci brought. You saw how the baby monkey likes shiny things."

"That's a—" He paused. "A really good idea."

"Okay, but you need to decorate superfast," Kimani told Joy.

"You poke bits of sea glass into this seedpod," Joy told Daniel. "And I'll stab berries onto these twigs while Kimani makes the counterweight."

After a couple of minutes, Joy stepped back from her creation. A curved stick stretched across the top of the monkey swing. The glass-decorated seedpod dangled from the stick beside a cluster of berries and a few shirt-buttons hanging from threads. Bright parrot feathers hung from the stick, along with flowers and colorful leaves.

"You made a baby mobile!" Daniel said.

"Yeah," Joy said.

"That's awesome."

She blushed. "It's okay."

"It's amazing," Kimani said, sitting with her legs dangling over the other side of the platform beside the empty swing.

"Are you done?" Daniel asked her.

Using some items she had stowed in her backpack, Kimani showed him the old shirt that she knotted into a sack to hold nuts, bolts, and rocks. "This should work as a counterweight. It's pretty heavy. Just make sure you keep the vine steady when I put it into the empty swing."

Daniel didn't know what that meant, so he said, "Let's switch places. You hold the vine and I'll drop the weight."

"Daniel's good at dropping things," Joy said. "He once dropped a whole blueberry pie."

"That's such a lie!" he said. "It was blackberry."

Kimani stood up and steadied the vine while Joy lowered the swing—with the baby mobile bobbing and dancing inside—down toward the monkey in the swamp.

Daniel sat motionless beside the empty swing on the other side of the platform. He held the counterweight in his lap, waiting for his big moment.

"Let's hope the decorations work." Joy's breath caught when the adult monkeys started shrieking again.

Daniel couldn't see the forest floor from where he was sitting. "What's happening?"

"The snake slithered into the water. She spotted the baby. Quicker, quicker!"

Kimani lowered the swing faster toward the little monkey, letting the slippery vine slide through her fingers.

"Slower, slower!" Joy said.

Daniel picked up the counterweight as he watched the baby's swing dropping slowly toward the forest floor. He wanted to be ready.

"Okay," Joy said to Kimani. "Go fast again. There!"

The swing landed a few feet from the monkey— and the colorful feathers, berries, and buttons of Joy's mobile bounced and fluttered cheerily.

"Ooh, the monkey's looking at the swing," Kimani said. "It likes all the flowers and stuff."

"Tell me when to drop the counterweight," Daniel said, worried that he'd mess up.

"I will," Kimani promised.

"C'mon, baby monkey," Joy called. "Come and get it!"

"Shush!" Daniel said. "You're scaring it."

"It can't hear me with the other monkeys chattering like that."

"If it can't hear you, why are you talking to it?"

"Because," she explained, before hollering again. "Climb into the pretty elevator. Hurry up!"

When the baby monkey started crawling toward

the swing, Daniel gripped the sack-shirt tightly, ready to drop the weight in the empty swing over the side the instant Kimani told him.

"The baby's so close," she said. "But there's the anaconda."

Daniel groaned when the snake's head broke the surface of the water near the tree. "What's the monkey doing?"

"It's—it's licking the swing," Joy said.

"Dumb monkey," Danial muttered.

"The snake's looking around!" Joy wailed. "She smells the monkey!"

"Bad anaconda!" Kimani threw a flip-flop from her backpack at the snake. "Go away!"

"She's not going away," Joy said.

Daniel's stomach knotted as the snake started toward the monkey. "She spotted the baby! Oh no..."

The other monkeys made an incredible racket, shrieking and squealing and screaming as the anaconda approached the baby monkey.

"The baby smells the fruit," Kimani reported. "The snake's only a few feet behind..."

Daniel stared in horror as the snake slithered closer. His fists clenched around the counterweight.

He didn't want to watch, but he couldn't look away as the anaconda closed in on the baby monkey.

Then a burst of green and blue flashed through the forest, as fast as a lightning bolt. Aiming right at the monkey and the snake!

"DaVinci!" Daniel screamed.

With a powerful flap of his wings, DaVinci bumped the baby into the swing, then rocketed upward away from the snake.

"He did it!" Joy screamed. "Yes!

"Now, Daniel!" Kimani yelled. "Now now *now*!"

Daniel placed the counterweight in the empty swing and lowered it over the edge of the platform.

Chapter 14

The counterweight worked perfectly. The swing with the sack of bolts and rocks plummeted to the ground as the baby swing attached to the other side of the vine swept upward fast.

But not too fast, not with Kimani keeping the vine steady.

The swing didn't even overturn when the goofy little baby started rocking the whole thing back and forth by reaching for the feathers, then the shiny leaves, then the berries on the little mobile.

When the swing reached Joy and Kimani, Daniel crossed the platform to join them. He peered inside and saw the fuzzy-headed baby munching happily on a handful of smooshed green fruit, like it had never been in any danger.

Daniel whispered, "So cute."

The monkey swiped at the decorated seedpod with the sea glass, making it spin merrily.

"I want to adopt a monkey," Joy said, her voice soft with awe.

"I want to adopt a parrot," Daniel said, though he couldn't tear his gaze away. "DaVinci's my hero."

"He's part of the team," Kimani said.

"He deserves his own headband!"

When they laughed, the baby monkey took the fruit out of its mouth and jabbered along.

"Can I hold it?" Joy asked.

Kimani tugged her ponytail. "I don't think that's a good idea."

"But we just saved its life," Joy said, and reached for the baby.

A chorus of shrieks cut through the quiet evening forest, and the troop of monkeys landed on the platform with a *tump tump tump*. They hooted and paced and glared at the kids. One or two bared their teeth, which looked pretty... toothy.

The monkeys were small, and the baby was adorable, but they were still wild animals.

Daniel felt his stomach drop. "Uh..."

"Let's move away from the baby," Kimani said softly.

Joy didn't say anything for once and just backed off.

Kimani and Daniel followed her across the platform while the monkeys grimaced and grunted and gestured. Then the mother monkey darted forward to gather the baby in her arms. The little fuzz-headed monkey clung to her happily.

"Aww," Daniel said.

"Yeah," Kimani said.

For a long moment they just stood there, watching the monkeys' reunion. Then the other monkeys must've smelled the fruit in the swing, because they began screeching and threatening again, pacing back and forth, showing their teeth. Like they didn't want to share.

DaVinci flew away with a squawk and Kimani told the monkeys, "Okay, okay, we're leaving."

"I'm glad you got your baby back!" Joy told the mother monkey.

"C'mon," Daniel said, trotting around the tree

trunk to the other side of the platform where the final zipline waited.

While Joy checked the knots, Daniel and Kimani looked toward the setting sun. Yellow light slanted through the leaves, giving the rainforest a warm glow. It was pretty, but it meant that evening was coming fast.

"All set!" Joy said. "Let's go!"

"Don't rush," Daniel told her.

"We're out of time, and the tower's like—" She squinted through the trees. "Ten blocks away."

"How far is that?" Kimani asked. "A few miles? I live in the suburbs, we don't have blocks!"

"It's far enough that we need to rush," Joy said.

"It'll take even longer if we fall and break our heads," Daniel said.

"Heads are overrated," Joy said, and leaped off the platform.

She zipped to the next tree, hooting and hollering like a monkey. Daniel and Kimani followed her, whizzing through the forest.

"DaVinci!" the parrot called, wheeling around them in the air. "Ahoy!"

Just as the sun touched the horizon, they reached the final platform.

Joy hopped impatiently. "Let's go, let's go!"

"Go where?" Daniel asked.

She pointed to the ground. "Look, no swamp! We can climb down and run to the tower."

The final platform wasn't high in the overstory, or the forest canopy. It should've been easy to reach the forest floor from the understory. It should've been quick. But the branches of the last tree were too far apart.

Instead of climbing down the tree like an oversized ladder, Daniel and Kimani lowered themselves carefully to the branches below. Then together they helped Joy, because she wasn't tall enough to reach—and because if they didn't, she'd try to leap from limb to limb like a monkey.

"I wish I had a tail," Joy said as Daniel helped her to the ground.

"I wish I had a flashlight," Daniel said, looking around at the gloomy, dark forest floor.

"Uh-oh," Joy said. "The sun's already down."

"Not totally," Kimani said. "Not yet."

"We're too far away though! We'll never get to the tower in time."

"We..." Daniel swallowed. "We failed."

Chapter 15

Kimani tugged unhappily on her necklace. "You're right. There's no way to reach the tower before the sun sets completely."

"We need to keep going," Daniel said as DaVinci landed on his shoulder. "And get out of the forest while there's still a little light."

"Before the shadows and shivers and falls," Kimani said in a little voice.

The air already felt cooler to Daniel, but he wasn't shivering. Not yet. As monkeys chattered behind him—maybe saying thanks, but probably just enjoying the smooshed fruit—he and the others hiked out of the rainforest.

A grassy field fell away to the right, brushed by the orange sunset. In the distance, the light glinted on the ocean. The pointy hill with the tower was straight ahead, and past that Daniel thought he saw sand dunes in the twilight.

The dunes were cool, but he spotted something even better on the twilit path ahead.

"A monkey fruit tree!" he said, peering through the shadows. "Finally! I've been wanting to eat one of those for hours."

"How can you be hungry?" Joy asked.

"That was a lot of exercise," he said, trotting ahead.

"But we failed," Joy moaned. "The sun's setting and we're a mile from the tower."

"Yeah," Kimani said, her shoulders slumping. "I guess we messed up."

Daniel reached for the lowest fruit on the tree. "Do you think the drummer will be mad?"

"Not at all," a woman's voice said. "I think she'll be very proud."

Daniel yelped in surprise as DaVinci squawked, "Ahoy!"

"Hey!" Joy blurted to the woman, who was barely visible on the path beyond the tree. "Where'd you come from?"

Daniel peered into the shadows. "Are you the mysterious drummer?"

"He means, are you the person who brought us here?" Kimani added.

"Yes, I suppose I am," the woman said, with laughter in her voice. "And I'm very pleased to meet you at last."

"But—how?" Daniel asked. "I mean, why? I mean, how and why?"

"Also," Joy said, "hi! I'm Joy and that's my cousin Daniel and our friend Kimani."

"Oh, I know who you are," the woman said. She seemed to float along the path toward them.

Daniel couldn't quite tell, but he thought he saw a tricorn hat atop her head with waves of black hair underneath it. And though he couldn't make out the colors in the gloom, she wore baggy clothes with a wide belt and her pants were tucked into high boots.

"Way!" DaVinci called, launching from Daniel's shoulder and landing on the woman's.

"That's right," the woman said, scratching the

parrot's chin. "I'm Captain Wei."

"You're a pirate from the shipwreck!" Joy said.

Daniel frowned. The woman *did* look like a pirate, but calling her one might not be polite. So he said, "The *captain* from the shipwreck."

The woman laughed. "That was one of my ships, yes. I commanded an entire fleet—and I've never been prouder of a crew than I am of you today."

"We're a crew," Kimani said softly, her eyes shining in the sunset.

"Of course we are," Joy said. "We even have the headbands."

"You work together to solve problems," the captain told them. "You try different methods, different solutions. You try and try and try, until you finally succeed."

"But we didn't succeed today," Kimani said.

Joy toed the ground. "We didn't make it to the tower in time."

"We had to save a baby monkey," Daniel explained.

"That's why I'm so proud," the captain said, her musical voice filling the evening. "I called for aid, for help in saving these magical islands. For a crew who'd work together to solve problems—but you didn't merely rise to the challenge I set."

"We didn't?" Joy asked.

"You made a better choice: you saved the monkey. You cared about what really matters. Not the task, but the islands and those who live here."

"It was *soooo* cute," Joy said.

"There is a greater challenge in store for you," Captain Wei said. "A far greater challenge. Once you reach the tower, I'll explain."

"Explain now!" Joy said. "What kind of challen—"

A hooting interrupted her. A rhythmic yelp and howl that echoed from the rainforest as the troop of monkeys shouted at them—probably jealous that Daniel had found a whole fruit tree for himself.

"Ooo—ooo—OO!" the monkeys howled. "Oooo! Oo-oo-OOOO!"

DaVinci launched from the captain's shoulder. He circled the fruit tree and called, "Oom! Boo-DOOM boom!"

"No," Joy said. "Not the drumbeat, not *now*!"

"I haven't eaten any monkey fruit yet!" Daniel cried.

"Please wait," Kimani said to Captain Wei. "Don't send us back before you explain."

"I can shape the island's magic, but I cannot control it," the captain told Kimani, a note of apology in her voice. "Apparently it's time for you to leave."

From the rainforest, the fluting song of night birds joined the monkey's chorus—*twee-diddee-tee OOO-oo- OOOO*—and a wind rose, shaking the leaves on the tree like maracas.

"Thoom-BOOM," DaVinci called. "Ooom-booda-boom!"

Drums sounded from the thickening darkness, pounding and exultant:

Boom-badoom-doom-boom-ba-BOOM.

Boom!

Boom-ba-doom-doom. Boom-ba-doom.

BOOM!

"I'm not ready!" Joy said, taking Kimani's hand. "I want to see the castle!"

Kimani squeezed Joy's hand. "We'll be back."

"You certainly shall," the captain's voice said. "I still need your help..."

"See you soon!" Kimani called to her friends.

"We'll miss you," Daniel told her.

The world spun around him, a blur of sunset and darkness. Then the drumbeat swallowed him like a hungry anaconda. He couldn't hear the monkeys or DaVinci, and he couldn't smell the swamp or the fruit tree.

He spiraled through the darkness like he was whizzing along the ziplines. Then he fell the final few feet... into the elevator in Joy's building.

She was standing in front of him—wearing her headband and stretching her arm out, like she was still holding Kimani's hand.

"Whoa," he said.

She closed her hand. "Ziplines!"

"Yeah."

"Monkeys!"

"Yeah."

"And a pirate captain," she said.

"Well, a captain," he said. "We don't know if she's a pirate."

"A pirate *queen*," Joy said. "But what did she mean, she needs our help?"

"No idea."

"I wish Kimani could've come home with us."

"Yeah."

Joy sighed. "What do you think she's doing now?"

"Writing everything down in her notebook," Daniel said. "The rainforest, the ziplines, the monkeys, the counterweight, the friction..."

"The *beautiful* anaconda."

Daniel smiled. "Yeah, and the fruit tree. I can't believe I never got a taste!"

"Maybe next time," she said.

"Next time," Daniel said, "for sure."

ARE YOU UP TO THE CHALLENGE?

Yo ho ho, buccaneers! Arrr ye ready for your Anaconda Swamp Challenge? That scallywag baby monkey up in the branches is getting antsy again. Before long, he'll be landin' his fuzzy tail back in the swamp. This time, it's up to YOU to keep him from becoming anaconda bait!

Yer challenge is to build a playground up in the rainforest's canopy layer where a baby monkey can play safely. You'll make a model monkey to test your designs and build an emergency rescue pulley just in case it escapes to the swamp. Joy, Kimani, and Daniel are here to help you map yer course for the challenge. Now full STEAM ahead into the rainforest!

KIMANI'S RAINFOREST STORIES

Did someone say STEAM? Because this rainforest is super steamy. It's like being in a bathroom right after a hot shower—24/7! The warm, wet climate makes it a perfect place for trees and plants to grow... and grow and grow and grow. Some rainforest trees grow up to 250 feet tall. That's about as tall as the Statue of Liberty!

In fact, just about everything that grows in the rainforest is supersized. There are fruits the size of ponies, flowers as big as monster truck wheels, and leaves as tall as pro basketball stars. Many rainforest animals are supersized too. There are spiders the size of soccer balls, butterflies the size of puppies, and snakes as long as a school bus!

Four Layers of Life

The rainforest is such an ideal spot for plants and animals to grow and thrive that more than half of the world's plant and animal species can be found there. How can one place be such a perfect match for so many different kinds of living things? The rainforest is actually made up of four completely different **habitats** stacked on top of one another. Each of the rainforest's four main layers (or stories) gets a different amount of sunlight and rain, making it a perfect home to a unique collection of plants and animals.

The **Emergent Layer**, also called the **Overstory**, is the top of the rainforest world and the sunniest spot in the jungle. More than two hundred feet above the ground, the overstory trees pop out over the rest of the jungle like green umbrellas. You have to be a good flyer or glider to live in this skyscraping layer. Overstory inhabitants include blue morpho butterflies, tiny pygmy bats, and the legendary harpy eagle, a super predator that swoops down and snags monkeys or pigs out of the lower jungle layers.

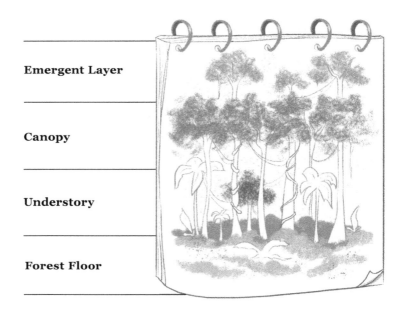

| Emergent Layer |
| Canopy |
| Understory |
| Forest Floor |

About 100 feet above the ground is the **Canopy**. The canopy is where most trees of the rainforest come together into a twenty-foot-deep maze of leaves and branches. Filled with yummy fruits, nuts, leaves, and insects, the colorful canopy is home to more animals than any other rainforest layer. Some of the rainforest's most iconic animals live in the canopy, including toucans, sloths, red-eyed tree frogs, and spider monkeys!

Beneath the canopy is the shadowy **Understory**. With only specks of light managing to peek through the dense canopy above, the understory makes a perfect home and camouflage for speckled predators like ocelots and leopards, as well as boa constrictors and pythons. But some brightly colored animals live there too, like poison dart frogs and all kinds of flashy birds and bugs.

Finally, we reach the **Forest Floor**, the rainforest's deep, dark lowest layer that sees only 2 percent of the sunlight shining down on the jungle. Many of the rainforest's most feared inhabitants live on the forest floor: army ants swarm by the millions and devour the flesh of anything in their path; jaguars prowl with razor-sharp teeth; and, of course, big, beautiful anacondas slither across the forest floor minding their own business... until they catch prey, which they squeeze then swallow whole!

JOY'S MONKEY TALES

Don't worry, Challenge Island friends, Kimani says there has never been a proven case of an anaconda eating a person. And while I can admit that all that swarming, chomping, squeezing, and swallowing does sound a wee bit gory, it's really just the rainforest food chain working in perfect harmony.

The good news for rainforest animals is that they are built to survive in a jungle of hungry predators. In fact, every animal in the rainforest is there because it has something special about it that helps protect it from becoming someone's dinner (or breakfast or lunch or midnight snack). These special features are called **adaptations**.

The red-eyed tree frog, for example, has an adaptation that allows it to scare predators away with (you guessed it!) its big red eyes. The capybara (an enormous but adorable rainforest rodent) has its eyes, nose, and mouth on the top of its head. This adaptation allows it to hide almost totally underwater and still breathe! And in case that capybara ever needs to hide all the way underwater, it has another adaptation that allows it to hold its breath for up to five minutes!

And those cute spider monkeys that Daniel, Kimani, and I met on our adventure have a handy adaptation too. It's called a **prehensile tail** and it's completely unique to monkeys of the rainforest. A prehensile tail acts as an extra arm and hand for canopy primates, providing essential backup protection as they swing from branch to branch and tree to tree. With the help of this adaptation, many rainforest monkeys live out their entire lives without ever setting hand, foot, or tail on the dark and dangerous forest floor. No wonder that little baby monkey's family was so upset to see it stumbling around in the swamp!

Now it's time to make your own baby monkey with a prehensile tail—perfect to use when you test out the playground you design later in the engineering process.

Make a Baby Monkey

Supplies

- Scissors
- Monkey template (download and print at www.challenge-island.com/books)
- Crayons or markers
- 3 pipe cleaners
- Tape
- Glue

Directions

1. Use the scissors to cut out the template of the two monkey shapes—a front and a back.

2. Color the front and back of your monkey with crayons or markers.

3. Turn over your monkey's back so that the colored side is facedown on the table. Place two pipe cleaners in an X over the center of the monkey's back and tape them down. These are the arms and legs.

4. Take the third pipe cleaner and place it so that it's pointing down from the middle of the X. Tape it in place. This is the tail.

5. Turn over your monkey's front so that the colored side is facedown on the table. Put glue all over the blank side, then stick it on top of the pipe cleaners on the blank side on the monkey's back. Be sure to match up the head and the sides, and then press it together.

Now your monkey's arms, legs, and tail are ready to wrap around the trees, branches, and playground equipment you build.

DANIEL'S MONKEY PLAYGROUND GAME PLAN

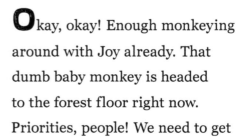

Okay, okay! Enough monkeying around with Joy already. That dumb baby monkey is headed to the forest floor right now. Priorities, people! We need to get that monkey playground built up in the canopy layer before our fuzzy-wuzzy friend turns into a fuzzy-wuzzy *wasn't!* First, let's round up some supplies.

Make a Monkey Playground

Supplies

Help protect the environment by using as many recycled products as you can!

- 2 kitchen chairs
- Broom or long pole
- Duct tape
- Green and brown streamers
- Flowers, leaves, bananas, or other fruit

- Pencil, pens, or markers
- Paper (regular or construction) or cardstock (or cut-up file folders or boxes)
- Scissors
- Optional items: empty cardboard tubes; colorful pipe cleaners; different-sized paper cups; recycled soda cans; lightweight odds and ends like paper coin wrappers or buttons; stuffed animals and/or pictures of rainforest animals; flowers, leaves, and bananas
- Yarn, ribbon, or paper clips
- Your model Baby Monkey

Set the STEAM Scene!

Your monkey playground will be set in the colorful and leafy rainforest canopy and suspended over a snake-infested forest floor. First, arrange the chairs so they are back to back and about three feet apart, then place a broom across the tops of the chairs. This will be the branch! If your broom branch feels too

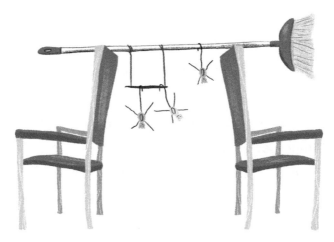

wobbly, duct tape it in place or lay it across the seats instead.

I know what you're thinking: this doesn't look like a rainforest! It looks like a broom and a couple of chairs. Luckily, DaVinci just swooped in with some tips for adding more A into your STEAM scene!

DaVinci's
Art Attack

Avast, lads and lassies! It's time to fly yer colors! Decorate your chairs and broom with green and brown streamers to make them look like trees and branches. Add fruits, flowers, and stuffed animals, if you dare. Then make yer forest floor as terrifyin' as Davy Jones's locker. Use streamers to make anacondas, crocodiles, and tarantulas. Make sure your monkey says, "Shiver me timbers!" when it looks down.

Brainstorm and Sketch Your Design!

Huddle up, Challenge Island team, because every winning design starts with a winning **brainstorm**. What kinds of swings and playground gear do you use at school or the park? We're talking tire swings, trapeze bars, gym rings, horse gliders, ladders, rope swings, saucer swings, disc swings, flat swings, and even baby swings. Now think about other kinds of high-up playground equipment you've seen—things like ziplines, horizontal ladders, rope bridges, hammocks, or even pirate ship swings! Can you think of other playground gear monkeys might enjoy? How about a telescope, a ship's wheel, a crow's nest, or even a monkey snack bar?

Remember how much the baby monkey liked butterflies, shiny objects, and yummy fruit? You can include those in your playground designs too. Let your imagination run as wild as the animals of the rainforest, then **sketch** all your great ideas on a piece of paper.

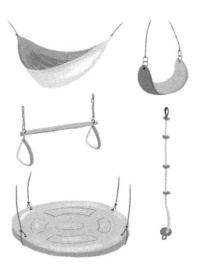

Build Your Playground!

It's finally time to bring your ideas to life! Use your sketches and trace them onto paper or cardstock, then color and cut them out. Collect different materials— like cardboard tubes, pipe cleaners, paper cups, recycled soda cans, and more—to build the greatest monkey playground ever! Hang your swinging creations from the tree branch using yarn, ribbon, or even paper clips. Use your model baby monkey to test out your designs for function and safety. Add new inspiration and ideas as they come. Make more baby monkeys to join in the fun!

KIMANI'S PULLEY POWER

Impressive work! The monkeys of the rainforest are now safer and happier because of your engineering and imagination! But good engineers also figure out solutions in case things don't work out exactly as planned. Like what if the baby monkey somehow ended up on the forest floor anyway? You would need an emergency rescue plan—or in this case, an emergency rescue pulley!

A **pulley** is a simple machine that makes it easier for people to lift things. The pulley was invented thousands of years ago by Archimedes, an ancient Greek mathematician, physicist, engineer, astronomer, philosopher, and all-around brilliant dude. A fixed pulley uses a rope on a wheel that has a weight on one end and a **counterweight** on the other. When the counterweight is heavier than the weight you are trying to raise, the pulley does the lifting work for you. Cool machines like elevators and cranes use pulley systems.

Daniel, Joy, and I used a pulley to save the baby monkey from the hungry anaconda. Since there weren't any wheels in the rainforest, we used a slippery vine over a tree platform instead. There was barely any friction between the vine and the platform, so our pulley system worked like a charm, even without a wheel. You can make an emergency rescue pulley for your monkey playground in the exact same way.

Make a Rescue Pulley

Supplies

- String or ribbon
- Scissors
- 1 empty toilet paper roll
- Tape
- 2 pipe cleaners
- 2 small paper cups
- Your model Baby Monkey
- Plastic pony beads
- 12 pennies

Directions

1. Look at your monkey playground and measure the distance from the floor to your tree branch using a piece of string. Cut it so that the string is a little longer than that distance.

2. Tape the toilet paper roll to the top of one of the chairs, near the tree branch.

3. To make the baskets, attach pipe cleaner handles to the paper cups. You can tape the pipe cleaners to the sides of the cups, or make two small holes at the tops of the paper cups and poke pipe cleaners through and twist them in place.

4. Make one of the baskets into a monkey baby swing by dangling a colorful mobile made of beads and string across the top of the pipe cleaner. The other basket will be your counterweight basket.

5. Tie one end of your string to the handle of the counterweight basket, and thread the other end through the cardboard tube. Then tie the other end of the string to the baby swing's handle.

6. Put your baby monkey in the baby swing basket with two pennies. The baby swing should now be on the forest floor.

7. To rescue your monkey, add ten pennies to the counterweight basket. Watch your baby monkey rise up to safety!

HELP SAVE THE RAINFOREST WITH JOY

Daniel, Kimani, and I know magic when we see it, and believe you me—rainforests are 100 percent magical, from the bottom of the forest floor to the top of the tallest tree, and every magical inch in between. Sadly, the rainforests of the world—and all the amazing animals and plants that call them home—are in great danger.

Every six seconds, a soccer field–sized area of tropical rainforest is destroyed. The trees are made into lumber and paper. The rich rainforest soil is mined for minerals, metals, and gems. Humans clear huge areas of the land to plant crops and raise cattle. They build roads and houses where the trees once stood.

The animals and plants of the rainforest have evolved and adapted to live there. Many rainforest species are not found anywhere else in the world. As rainforests disappear, so do the plants and animals that lived in them.

The good news is that there are things we kids can do to help protect the earth's tropical ecosystems. Here are a few of my favorite ideas for making a difference:

- **Reduce, reuse, and recycle**. If you can use less, you'll make less waste! Reuse old products for new purposes instead of throwing them out, just like we did in the swamp and rainforest. After all, you can make some cool stuff with empty toilet paper rolls! Help save trees by recycling paper products and buying recycled paper. Recycle aluminum cans since one of the ingredients used to make them (bauxite) is mined from rainforest soil.

- **Hold a rainforest sundae bar fundraiser.** Some of the yummiest ingredients for ice cream sundaes come from the rainforest, like bananas, pineapples, cinnamon, vanilla beans, cacao beans (chocolate), and coconut. Ask your teacher if you can organize a rainforest sundae bar fundraiser for your class. Each student can bring a different ingredient plus a small donation for the cause. Send the money you raise to an organization that helps protect the rainforest. You can research some organizations you like, but here are a few good ones:

Rainforest Alliance, www.rainforestalliance.org

Rainforest Trust, www.rainforesttrust.org

- **Share the magic**. The more people know about the magic of the rainforests, the more they care about them and the harder they work to protect them. So spread the word! Tell your friends and family about all the amazing creatures and wildlife that live in the rainforest layers. If you use social media, post pictures of adorable rainforest animals with the hashtag #SaveTheRainforest. Have a recycled art party and use the items in your recycling bin to design different kinds of rainforest plants and animals. Enroll in a Challenge Island Rainforest Island class and do more exciting STEAM-based rainforest projects. The possibilities are as unlimited as your imagination!

Share Your Creations!

Once you finish building your monkey playground and emergency rescue pulley, share your cool creations with other Challenge Island kids! Send your photo to Books@challenge-island.com and we'll post it on our website at www.challenge-island.com.

STEAMtastic work, lads and lassies! You've completed the Anaconda Swamp Challenge! But there are many more islands awaiting our arrival filled with puzzles to solve and challenges to conquer. The future is in your hands, head and imagination.

So, until next time...

Boom-ba-DOOM-boom-boom badoom.

With over 100 locations in the USA and worldwide, Challenge Island has enriched the lives of more than 1 million children in over 6000 schools and community organizations. Its classes, camps, field trips, and scout workshops take kids on STEAMtastic learning adventures in settings such as Time Machine Island, Mythology Island, Rainforest Island, and Sharktooth Island. Wrapped in whimsical trimmings (colorful headbands, team spirit, and the beat of the Challenge Island drum), kids work together to tackle challenges, using only a treasure chest full of low-tech supplies and their boundless imaginations.

Learn more about the Challenge Island program at www.challenge-island.com

CPSIA information can be obtained
at www.ICGtesting.com
Printed in the USA
BVHW051646020522
635895BV00001B/1